Anonymous

In Memoriam

John White Geary

Anonymous

In Memoriam
John White Geary

ISBN/EAN: 9783337092603

Printed in Europe, USA, Canada, Australia, Japan

Cover: Foto ©Raphael Reischuk / pixelio.de

More available books at **www.hansebooks.com**

In Memoriam.

PHILADELPHIA:
1873.

From the Press of W. W. Bates & Co.

John White Geary.

—

Born December 30th. 1819.

Died February 8th. 1873.

WE, the surviving Staff-Officers of MAJOR GENERAL JOHN W. GEARY, during the late War, deeming it our duty,—record as our tribute to the military character and services of our dead Commander, this

Memorial.

In presenting this we shall avoid all eulogy; confining ourselves to the recital of facts known to us, and to the expression of opinions formed from daily intercourse with him, in the camp, on the battle-field and under circumstances that not only try "mens' souls," but lay bare their thoughts and their motives.

We knew him as no others could, save his own family. Some of us entered the service under his command in 1861, and the majority of us were members of his staff in 1865 when the war closed. We therefore speak what we know; and we wish our country to know him somewhat as we knew him.

He was ambitious—but he was patriotic.

He sought distinction—but he loved his country.

He was prudent and careful—but he was brave.

Naturally high tempered,—his temper was generally under good control; under great excitement, he was sometimes unjust,—but he was generous,—quick to acknowledge a wrong and prompt to make reparation.

He was vigilant and unwearied in the performance of his duty.

We but quote the often expressed estimate of his Commanding Generals, when we say that as a Division Commander he had few equals and no superiors.

This estimate was due partially to that strict military discipline which led him to yield prompt, unquestioned obedience to his superiors, and to expect, without excuse, obedience of the same character from all under his command; as well as by his unceasing personal watchfulness over the condition and movements of every Staff Department, and of even the smallest body of troops under his command.

He never permitted his troops to be unfurnished with material or supplies; No matter at what hour of the day or night came the order to march, the White Star Division was ready. This became proverbial in the Army, and that it was so, was due to the unceasing personal vigilance of the only Commander it ever had—John W. Geary.

Whatever of success and reputation was achieved by the White Star Division, its inspiration, support and development came from but one Commander; the material which composed it abounded in the qualities that mark the highest type of the American volunteer soldier, but these qualities were developed and utilized to the best advantage by one leader.

He timed his marches and his halts with wonderful judgment, so as not to unnecessarily fatigue his troops; bringing them to camp, or into action in good order and condition.

On the march, he habitually rode in advance, selected personally the camping ground for his troops, disposing them with special view to convenience of wood and water, and security for the night; and long after his subordinates, wearied to exhaustion, were sound asleep by their camp fires, General Geary, attended by a single Staff-officer, might often be found making the rounds of his lines to see that all was right.

In battle the same qualities were prominent. Without recklessly exposing his troops, he was vigilant, always ready, prompt to take every advantage offered, and firm as the rocks in holding a position he had gained.

During the war he never allowed his command to be surprised or taken at a disadvantage, and he was never driven from a position, nor ever failed of success.

To tell the record of the 2nd Division 20th Army Corps,—and from its organization known by its badge, as the White Star Division,—is but to repeat four years of General Geary's biography. The reputations of both are interdependent. One cannot be wounded without injury to the other.

Of General Geary's military career during the Mexican war, and of his honorable record from the 28th of July, 1861, until the 9th of August, 1862, when he was dangerously wounded at the battle of Cedar Mountain, we do not deem it our province to speak at length.

During the first twelve months of the late war he was assigned an independent command, comprising the 28th Penna. Vols., and Knap's Battery, with other battalions of infantry and cavalry, his work being to guard the upper Potomac, including the adjacent counties of

Virginia and Maryland, as far south as the line of the Rappahannock.

From the 15th of July, to the 9th of August, 1862, he commanded the 1st Brigade of Auger's Division in Pope's Army of Virginia.

His command of this Brigade terminated with the battle of Cedar Mountain, where his left arm was completely shattered by a bullet, and he was compelled to return home for treatment. Although urged by surgeons to submit to amputation, he refused, and by the first of October was with the Army of the Potomac, then encamped around Harper's Ferry, after the battle of Antietam, in which his Brigade had borne its full share; this battle was the only one among the many in which his troops were engaged during the war, at which General Geary was not present in command. Shortly before Antietam, Auger's Division with the rest of Pope's Army had become part of the Army of the Potomac under McClellan, and about the time of General Geary's return, orders were issued reorganizing the Army. The 12th Corps was constituted under command of Major-General Slocum, and General Geary was assigned command of the 2nd Division, comprising his old Brigade, under Colonel Candy, the 2nd Brigade, under General Kane, and the 3rd Brigade, commanded by General Greene.

Shortly after, when General Hooker designated a separate badge to be worn by the troops of each Division, the "White Star" became the symbol of General Geary's

Division, and until the close of the war "in that sign" they conquered.

At Chancellorsville, the 12th was one of the four Corps heavily engaged. There, General Geary and his command, attacked from front, right and left, owing to the unfortunate disaster to the 11th Corps on his right, held the advanced position for hours against the repeated assaults of Lee's Army, and retired to the new line established for our Army, when there was barely a loop-hole of escape, dragging with them by hand the artillery of the Division; every horse belonging to the Batteries having been shot, and most of their Officers killed or wounded.

In this action General Geary's heroism and command of his troops were conspicuous, and he stood among them, brave and determined to the last. A solid shot from the enemy's cannon grazed him so closely as to produce a compression of his chest, rendering him voiceless for nearly two days, from the effects of which he never entirely recovered. Yet he remained in command, issuing his orders in whispers to his staff, throughout the entire battle.

At Gettysburg his ability and heroism were displayed on a wider field, and with those of other commanders were crowned with victory. During the preliminary action of the 1st of July, in which the Corps of Reynolds and Howard were unexpectedly engaged near Gettysburg, orders came to General Geary while resting his troops for dinner, at "Two Taverns," to push to the front. No time was lost. After seeing the troops well on their way, General Geary, with his Staff, rode rapidly ahead to Cemetery Hill, where he found the 1st and 11th Corps posted after their engagement, and General Hancock in temporary command as the Senior Officer on the field.

Hancock addressing Geary said: "You see the high "knoll on our left—(Round Top). If you can get your "troops there before the enemy gets possession, we can "establish a line and fight him here. That knoll is the "key to the position, and in the absence of General "Slocum, I will give you a direct order to take it—hurry "up your troops."

His Division was hastened forward, and when night fell had occupied Round Top, driving off the enemy's cavalry, and had stretched its attenuated line, connecting with the 11th Corps on Cemetery Hill.

During the night other Corps arrived and new dispositions were made; to the 11th Corps was given the right of the line fronting Rock Creek, and at daylight on the morning of the 2d, Geary's Division moved from the left to the right of the army line and occupied Culp's Hill; how that position was held during two days of battle that followed is matter of history, doubly attested by the timber which stands to this day seared and deadened by the tempest of lead.

One of the most critical periods in the great battle, was the night of the 2d and the morning of the 3d, when,

had General Geary and his Division less faithfully and
bravely performed their work, our army would have been
in imminent peril.

During all the 2d the enemy had made persistent
efforts to obtain a foothold on Culp's Hill, and further on
our right, evidently knowing that if he succeeded, he
would have possession of the Baltimore turnpike, and that
our defeat would be instant and overwhelming.

But every charge had been repulsed, and as night
gathered, he apparently relinquished his fruitless efforts.
Then came information that the left of the army line was
in danger of being overpowered, and orders to take to
the threatened point, as reinforcement, all of the 12th
Corps excepting one Brigade.

Geary's 3d Brigade, commanded by that sturdy and
heroic fighter, General Greene, was ordered to extend its
line to occupy the entire position held by the 12th Corps.
Silently, in the dusk of evening, Williams' Division of
the 12th Corps and the other two Brigades of Geary's
Division, filed out of their breastworks and across the
Baltimore turnpike towards the point designated—the
troops of Greene's Brigade stretching out not thicker than
a skirmish line to occupy the vacated works. But the
enemy had not relaxed his vigilance. Seeing his
opportunity he charged, and before Greene could fully
extend his line, was in possession of the works left by
Williams' Division. But Greene was equal to the
occasion; he formed the right of his Brigade to meet the

assault, holding the works in his front with a skirmish line, and fought with desperation, until Geary learned the situation, and hastened back to his relief.

With his remaining troops Geary connected with Greene and the enemy was repulsed, but remained in possession of our breastworks on Greene's right. Geary was sleepless that night, knowing that in the morning the enemy must be driven from that position or our army was defeated.

All night he worked posting troops and batteries. He planted 24 pieces of artillery, bearing upon the enemy's position—gave his personal attention to sighting the guns, taking certain trees as a guide for the gunners—he went repeatedly along the lines where his troops, and others which had been ordered to report to him, were massed near the Baltimore turnpike, crouching in silence, ready to spring to the assault.

At daylight, in accordance with General Geary's plan, his artillery opened and maintained its fire for thirty minutes; his infantry then charged;—the breastworks were retaken, and the line re-established; subsequently the enemy was driven across Rock Creek, and the victory of the army of the Potomac was assured; for generations to come, travellers visiting Culp's Hill, where this memorable rencontre occurred, will wonder how men could live where trees were stripped of their bark by the hailstorm of bullets on that eventful morning.

During the two days and three nights that General Geary spent upon the field of Gettysburg, he had scarcely two hours unbroken sleep; yet when the victory was won, on the fourth day he was in the saddle at sunrise and ready for a day's march of twenty miles, in pursuit of the enemy.

Scarcely had the armies of Meade and Lee resumed their old lines along the Rappahannock, when intelligence was received of the disaster to our arms at Chickamauga: and at once the Eleventh and Twelfth Corps were placed under the command of General Hooker, and dispatched to the relief of General Thomas at Chattanooga.

The battle of Wauhatchie, fought by only about 1500 men under the personal command of General Geary, on the night of the 28th of October, 1863, enabled our army to open the line of supplies by the Tennessee River, from Bridgeport to Chattanooga, and saved the almost starving Army of the Cumberland;—pursuant to Grant's plan for relieving the army, the greater portion of the Eleventh and Twelfth Corps had, by forced marches, reached Lookout Valley, and had encamped for the night at the foot of Lookout Mountain; the Eleventh Corps having the advance, occupied the hills skirting the Tennessee River; and at about five o'clock in the evening, General Geary having reached Wanhatchie, a position covering the road to Kelley's Ferry, bivouacked his command for a few hours rest;—all day long the enemy from his position on Lookout Mountain, 2500 feet above,

had watched the movements of our troops, and counted
their strength; regarding it as an easy night's work to
"gobble up a wagon guard" as he designated Geary's
command in his official report; one Division of Longstreet's
Corps, about 5000 strong, marched down in the darkness
in full confidence of victory;—drove in Geary's pickets;—
with exultant yells assaulted his little force, and by
superiority of numbers enveloped him on three sides.

But he had carefully made his dispositions, and was
not taken unprepared; well he knew that his defeat at
that point would result in almost irretrievable disaster to
the Army of the Cumberland; while victory would almost
insure its safety; neither troops nor commander could be
moved from their position; and after three hours of most
terrific midnight fighting, the enemy was driven in hasty
retreat back to Lookout Mountain, leaving on the field
in dead, wounded and prisoners, more than the entire
number of troops that General Geary had engaged.

Throughout that fearful contest, Geary's gallantry
was displayed in the highest degree; the loss of officers
in his command was unusually severe, and among those
killed was his son, Lieutenant Edward Geary of Knap's
Battery, a young officer of unusual promise, and beloved
by all who knew him; few could know the high hopes of
the father which were crushed in an instant by this terrible
blow; yet, though cognizant of the fact when it occurred,
for they were but a few feet apart, the father sunk the
fearful sense of personal bereavement, in that of duty to

his country, and nerved himself the more to the conflict.

General Hooker, in his official report of this action, says:

"During these operations, a heavy musketry fire with "occasional discharges of artillery, continued to reach us " from Geary; it was evident that a formidable adversary " had gathered around him, and that he was battering him " with all his might."

"For almost three hours, without assistance, he " repelled the repeated assaults of vastly superior numbers, "and in the end drove them ingloriously from the field; " at one time they had him enveloped on three sides, under " circumstances that would have dismayed any officer " except one endowed with an iron will and the most " exalted courage: such is the character of General " Geary."

It would be useless to indulge in speculations as to the possible results which might have ensued, had Geary been defeated in this action; it is enough to say that his success was deemed of the first importance by his commanding General, and the victory was hailed by General Thomas and his hungry Army in Chattanooga, as their sure deliverance from almost actual famine: the next day, steamers conveyed by the Tennessee River, provisions and forage to the Army of the Cumberland, enabling them to recuperate for their part in the series of brilliant achievements so soon to follow, and in all of which Geary and his command bore their full share.

The first of these,—the storming and capture of Lookout Mountain,—took place less than a month after Wauhatchie; and fully did Hooker appreciate the peculiar abilities of General Geary, when he selected him and about 2000 of the White Star Division to storm the heights from which the enemy had so long, in apparent security, observed the most secret movements of our Army; for it should be borne on record,—that this memorable assault was made alone by this small force headed by General Geary:—all the other troops under Hooker's command, being held as supports at the base of the mountain.

And here we quote again from General Hooker's official report:—after speaking of the other troops, of the scaling of the mountain and driving of the enemy by Geary and his command, the report says:

"This lasted until 12 o'clock, when Geary's advance "heroically rounded the peak of the mountain; not "knowing to what extent the enemy might be reinforced, "directions had been given for the troops to halt on "reaching this high ground; but fired by success,—with "a flying, panic-stricken foe before them, they pressed "impetuously forward; our success was uninterrupted "and irresistible; at a quarter past five o'clock, General "Carlin of the Fourteenth Corps, reported to me with "his Brigade, and was assigned to duty on the right of

"the line to relieve Geary's command almost exhausted
"with the fatigue and excitement incident to their
"unparalleled march."

During the next three days the memorable assault
upon Mission Ridge, in which Geary's Division lost some
of its bravest spirits; the battle of Ringgold, where Geary
and his Eastern troops vied with Osterhaus and his Western
heroes in gallantry and daring:—and the pursuit of Bragg
to the mountain wilds of Georgia completed the brief
campaign so brilliantly opened at Wauhatchie.

For the signal services of the White Star Division
in these operations, a special review of this Division alone,
was ordered by the Army Commander, at which were
present Generals Grant, Thomas, Hooker and Hunter,
with a majority of the Army and Corps Commanders of
the Department;—an honor accorded to very few if to
any other single Division during the war.

For his personal gallantry and services, Generals
Grant, Thomas and Hooker united in a recommendation
to the Secretary of War, that General Geary should be
made a Major General; the promotion was promised by
the Secretary so soon as a vacancy should occur in
Pennsylvania appointments, but the promise was never
fulfilled; General Geary however, did not relax in the
least, his zeal in the cause of his country; untiring in his
patriotism, during all the remaining months of the war he
marched and fought, devoting to her cause all the great
strength and wonderful energy of his nature.

About this time, an order of the War Department authorized the re-enlistment of troops who had served continuously for two years; and, in consideration of their re-engagement for an additional term of three years, conferred upon them, with other privileges, the honorary title of "Veterans." To this order, the first response came from the White Star Division; on the 9th day of December, 1864, the 29th Pennsylvania Volunteers were re-mustered into the service as the *First* Veteran Regiment of the war; the entire Division, including Knap's Battery, followed as rapidly as their musters could be made out; the single exception being that of the 7th Ohio Volunteers; this magnificent Regiment, one of the best in the Division, after serving three years and three months, and having been conspicuous for gallantry on every field, had but a few days before the receipt of the "Veteran" order, suffered fearfully at Ringgold where were killed its Colonel, Lieutenant Colonel, Adjutant, and a very large proportion of its line officers; the rank and file also suffered so severely that barely a "Corporal's Guard" of the Regiment was left; we believe this to be the only instance in the Army where an entire Division re-enlisted under the "Veteran" order.

On the 1st of May, 1864, commenced the campaign of Sherman against Atlanta, to end only when one hundred days of almost continuous battle had won for us that stronghold of the enemy; and into which the first national colors to be carried were those of the White Star

Division; in all the battles and marches of this campaign, General Geary and his Division bore a prominent part, and inscribed on their banners the legends, " Mill Creek Gap," " Resaca," " New Hope Church," "Pine Hill," " Kenesaw," " Peach Tree Creek," and scores of minor engagements.

After a brief rest in Atlanta, the " March to the Sea" followed, during which each Corps and Division of the Armies of Georgia and of the Tennessee vied with the other for the honor attaching to the capture of the enemy's cities; Savannah was the great prize; bravely, persistently was it contended for, and again, as at Atlanta, General Geary's Division took the honors, and the White Star was the first national emblem unfurled over the captured city.

For this achievement, General Geary was made Military Governor of Savannah, and here his peculiar administrative and executive ability was fully displayed; the City was quickly placed in the best sanitary condition; good order and personal security were guaranteed and enforced; and the people who had feared the approach of our Army were led to admire and respect it; so general was this feeling that a most respectful and powerful appeal was made by the residents of the city to the General Commanding, to have General Geary retained as their Governor when the Army should again advance; but he was known to be useful in the field as well as in the administrative chair, and the request was not granted.

Throughout the Carolinas, as upon all former campaigns, General Geary impressed upon all under his command, both by orders and personal example, that while the enemy should be fought bravely and persistently, no unnecessary distress should be caused to the unfortunate or the helpless; the campaign from Savannah to Raleigh was not marked by any severe engagements, but it called for as much energy, endurance and vigilance as did any during the war; and we can testify how strikingly all these qualities were manifested by General Geary; his engineering skill and personal supervision of details enabled him to overcome obstacles and to achieve results on that long and harrassing march through the swamps and quicksands of the Carolinas in mid-winter, when most other men would have failed; one great cause of his success in these operations was the promptness which characterized all his movements; his Division was never known to be a second behind the time ordered, whether to march,—to form in line of battle—or to charge the enemy; so prominent was this characteristic, that it was frequently said by his superior officers: "Order Geary to march at Four, and he'll be on the road at half past Three."

In reviewing this brief sketch, we feel that we have not been able in so short a space, to do more than present a few instances, among the hundreds that came under our observation, of the display of those leading qualities which made General Geary what he was; and with but few additional words we close our tribute;— General Geary was consistently and conscientiously a temperance man:—temperate in eating, and abstaining entirely from intoxicating drinks; his social relations were marked by a purity and a strength from which the temptations of the army could not swerve him; he was companionable by nature, and often did his social qualities render lighter and more easily borne, the hardships of the march and the deprivations of the camp; he was economical; and was in the habit of saving much of his salary and investing it in the securities of the Government.

At Murfreesboro, Stevenson, Bridgeport, and many other points, and conspicuously at Savannah, had he prostituted his position for money, or misused the opportunities presented to him while in command, he might have accumulated a fortune, but under all circumstances, his integrity was unsullied and unquestioned.

He acquired the confidence, and retained the affection of those who knew him most intimately, in a marked degree; from the organization of the White Star Division until the close of the war, his Staff remained continuously the same with such exceptions as were caused by death or promotion; no Staff Officer of his Division ever resigned or was dismissed.

Our feeling of unity with each other, and with our late commander is therefore a tie of more than ordinary character; the memories of our dead and the wounds of the living are silent and impressive witnesses to the truth of this tribute to the character of our Chief.

To his widow we dedicate this memorial, and ask the privilege of laying our chaplet upon the tomb of

JOHN WHITE GEARY.

WILLIAM T. FORBES,
Major and Ass't Adjutant General,
Bv't Lt. Col. U. S. Vols.

MOSES VEALE,
Major 109th P. V. V., Ass't Commissary Musters,
and A. D. C.

REUBEN H. WILBUR,
Major 102d N. Y. V. V., Ass't Commissary Musters,
and A. D. C.
Bv't Lt. Col. U. S. Vols.

LEWELLYN R. DAVIS,
Captain 7th Ohio V., and A. D. C.,
Lt. Col. 187th Ohio Vols.

JOHN P. GREEN,
Captain, Ass't Adjutant General U. S. V.
and A. D. C.

WILLIAM C. ARMOR,
Captain 28th P. V. V. and A. D. C.
Bv't Major U. S. Vols.

WILLIAM H. LAMBERT,
Captain 33rd N. J. V., and Ass't Inspector General,
Bv't Major U. S. Vols.

MICHAEL NOLAN,
Captain 69th N. Y. V. V., Acting Judge Advocate,
Bv't Major U. S. Vols.

EUGENE SCHILLING,

> Captain 102d N. Y. V. V., Topographical Engineer,
>> Bv't Major U. S. Vols.

ALFRED BALL,

> Surgeon 5th Ohio V. V., Surgeon in Chief.

J. A. WOLF,

> Surgeon 29th P. V. V., and Surgeon in Chief.

H. EARNEST GOODMAN,

> Surgeon U. S. V. Surgeon in Chief.
>> and Colonel U. S. Vols.

GILBERT L. PARKER,

> Captain and Ass't Quarter Master, U. S. V.,
>> Bv't Lt. Col. U. S.Vols.

JAMES GILLETTE,

> Captain and Commissary Subsistence U. S. V.,
>> Bv't Major 15th Infantry, U. S. A.

BENJ. F. LEE,

> Captain and Commissary of Subsistence, U. S. Vols.

JOSEPH A. MOORE,

> Captain 147th P. V. V., Ass't Comm'y Subsistence.

HENRY H. WILSON,
> Captain 147th P. V. V., and Ordnance Officer.

WILLIAM E. GOODMAN,
> Captain 147th P. V. and Ordnance Officer.
>> Bv't Maj. U.S. Vols.

CHARLES W. CHAPMAN,
> 1st Lieut. 28th P. V. V., and Ambulance officer.

WILLIAM J. MACKEY,
> Major 147th P. V. V., and Ambulance officer.